SAMSON THE SUPER DOG

WRITTEN AND ILLUSTRATED BY SARAH E WEBSTER

The Book Guild Ltd

First published in Great Britain in 2017 by
The Book Guild Ltd
9 Priory Business Park
Wistow Road, Kibworth
Leicestershire, LE8 0RX
Freephone: 0800 999 2982
www.bookguild.co.uk
Email: info@bookguild.co.uk
Twitter: @bookguild

Typeset in Century Gothic

Printed by Cambrian Print, Llandudno, Wales

ISBN 978 1911320 326

British Library Cataloguing in Publication Data.
A catalogue record for this book is available from the British Library.

For Bilbo
Cornwall's Real Lifeguard

www.bilbosays.com

Photo © Steve Jamieson

THIS BOOK BELONGS TO

....

Across the blue seas...

and   the   mountains...
over purple

through green fields...

1

and sunny lemon groves...

on a small Italian beach lived Samson, a very special dog and the hero of our story.

Samson was a very large type of dog called a Newfoundland, or 'Newfie' for short. He had chocolate brown fur, an enormous wagging tail and an even bigger heart. He was loyal, brave and had many friends. He was also a very good swimmer thanks to his large webbed feet, waterproof coat and incredible strength.

Every day Samson went for a morning swim in the cool water of his sunny bay. He would often race his friends in and out of the water and almost always came first.

One day, as Samson was drying off on the warm sand after a long morning swim, he noticed, out of the corner of his eye, another dog watching him from a distance. Samson immediately got up and shouted 'Hello!' to the other dog, who on hearing this greeting walked over.

'Mighty fine swimmer, aren't you,' said the other dog, who was also a Newfoundland. 'Couldn't help noticing that you have a very impressive stroke.'

'Why, thank you,' said Samson, a little embarrassed.

'My name is Rodolpho, by the way. Member of the Italian lifeguards, K9 division.'

'What's that?' asked Samson.

'Well, as a lifeguard dog, I help to teach other people on the beach about water safety and when I'm not doing that I do a lot of training, especially swimming, so I'm fit and ready in case there's an incident and someone needs rescuing.'

'Wow! That sounds like a great job to me!' said Samson, clearly impressed.

'Well, yes it is, actually. More to the point, we're looking for new recruits, and need young fellows like you, who are good, strong swimmers and are also friendly and approachable. In short, I'd like to invite you to come to our training school for young lifeguard dogs, where you'll learn all you need to know about beach safety and how to perform different rescues.'

Samson accepted Rodolpho's invitation at once and they both set off for the training school.

Samson spent many, many months training with his fellow pals until eventually, after much hard work he passed his exams in beach safety and the all-important fitness test too.

One day while Samson was practicing his rescues in the water with his fellow lifeguard team, Rodolpho appeared with two strange men dressed in bright red and yellow uniforms.

'Samson, I'd like you to meet Tom and John.'

'How do you do,' said Samson politely.

'They are interested in our school and how dogs like us can make successful beach lifeguards,' explained Rodolpho.

'That's right,' said Tom. 'We think our team in Cornwall could really benefit from your help and expertise, and are here to ask you to come to England with us, if you'd like to?'

Though Samson had been training for a very long time, he had never actually had a proper job as a lifeguard. This was his moment!

'I'd be honoured!' exclaimed Samson.

'That's great!' said John. 'Of course, you'll need to get a passport first and once all the paperwork has been arranged you'll then be free to travel with us to England.'

'But where will I stay?' asked Samson.

'You don't need to worry about that,' said Tom kindly. 'You can stay with us if you like.'

Samson was very excited, but he also knew deep down that he would be sad to leave Rodolpho and the others at the training school. He promised he would write to them at every opportunity and made them promise in return to visit him in England.

A few weeks later Samson's paws touched down on English soil at Newquay Cornwall Airport.

They then drove to Tom and John's house, a small stone cottage, which had a wonderful view of the beach. Tom and John showed Samson his bedroom, before having a lovely tea of fish, potatoes, and warm milk. As Samson bid them good night he went to sleep with the feeling that he'd be very happy here.

The next morning they all woke up bright and early and after a good breakfast headed down to the beach. It was a fine day. Samson could smell the salt of the sea and felt the fresh wind rippling through his fur coat. The sea sparkled in the sunlight and the waves calmly lapped the seashore.

Tom and John had put on their bright red and yellow uniforms to help them stand out on the beach. Then, seeing the water was calm and the weather fine, Samson put up two red and yellow flags to let people know it was safe to swim in that area. He then patrolled between the flags, chatting to people passing by and reminding them to put on their sunhats and sun cream and to swim between the flags, close to the beach.

Everyone who came down to the seaside enjoyed themselves. People were playing games, eating ice creams, splashing about in the sea and chatting to Samson, who would always give tips on how to stay safe on the beach.

Some days, Tom, John and Samson staged a rescue, where Samson would rescue Tom or John. People applauded loudly and after the demonstration the three lifeguards would explain how people could avoid getting into trouble in the water.

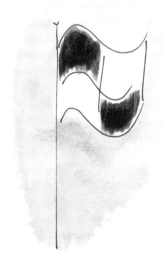

When the waves were big lots of surfers came down to the beach. On these days, Samson would raise the black and white chequered flags as well as the red and yellow ones to separate the surfers from the swimmers. When Samson was off duty, he was a pretty good surfer and people would clap and cheer as they saw him on his surfboard sweeping the crests of the waves.

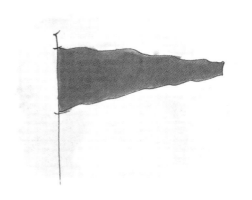

On other days, Samson would observe the strong winds and putting up the orange windsock, he would ask people with inflatable dinghies and floats to leave them on the beach, in case the wind carried them out to sea.

All was well… until one day, when the sky turned dark and stormy and the sea became rough and choppy. The rain was heavy and the wind howled, buffeting the little stone cottage. John had the flu, and was tucked up in bed and Tom had to attend an important lifeguard meeting away in Newquay. Today, Samson would have to go on duty alone.

He went down onto the beach first thing, his torpedo buoy around his shoulders. Seeing the terrible weather, Samson was quick to raise the red flags, which meant no swimming or surfing at all in the water. As he stood between the flags and looked up and down and all around him, he could see that the beach was deserted. The day was miserable – it was hardly surprising that everyone was staying indoors today. Samson, stoic and faithful as ever, remained at his post whilst the weather continued to worsen. Thunder rumbled overhead and the sea grew fiercer, as foam frothed and flew with every break of the waves.

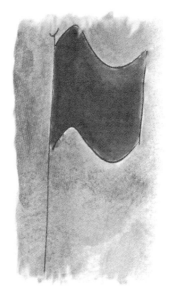

Suddenly, Samson saw a long white object floating into view from around the corner of the beach where jagged cliffs rose up into the sky. Something small and black was clinging to the object as the waves kept buffeting it. Samson immediately realised the object was a surfer clinging to his surfboard! 'The casualty must have been surfing in the cove around the corner from here, which is unpatrolled and unprotected by lifeguards!' he thought.

Samson, all alone, instantly knew what he had to do and all his training at the Italian school came back to him. Without a moment's hesitation Samson shouted to the stormy air, 'Lifeguard going in!' and plunged into the waves.

Using his tail as a big rudder to steer and his strong muscles and webbed paws, Samson powered through the cold waves, though he didn't feel at all cold, thanks to his warm undercoat. 'I'm coming, hold on!' shouted Samson to the surfer, who was still floundering in the rough waves. A few moments later, Samson was passing the surfer's shoulder.

'Take hold of my torpedo!' shouted Samson, and the surfer instantly gripped hold of the bright red rescue aid.

'Hold on tight!' said Samson, and manoeuvring carefully around to avoid the rocks and face the shore, he streaked forward. Samson swam as fast as he could against the current. As he approached the shore, the rain began to ease and the wind blew more softly.

People began to gather on the sand dunes, and Samson spotted Tom's yellow t-shirt and John wearing a large blanket amongst the crowd. Even an ambulance had arrived.

As Samson's paws felt the sand and he pulled his casualty the last few metres the crowd let out an almighty cheer with much clapping and many 'Hurrahs!'

'Thank you,' said the surfer, breathing heavily and patting Samson. 'You saved my life!'

The ambulance crew rushed forward to wrap the young surfer in blankets and check that Samson was alright too.

'Congratulations Samson,' said a paramedic, as she helped the surfer into the ambulance. 'Hear, hear!' exclaimed her colleague. 'You did a great job out there! Not many people could have swum that far or fast in these conditions.'

'Thanks, but I don't understand how you got here so fast?!' exclaimed Samson.

'That was me,' said John in between sneezing and coughing. 'I got up to make a cup of tea and looking out the window saw you rushing into the water. I called 999 straight away.'

'We really do make a great team, don't we,' said Samson, and Tom and John smiled.

'Extra fish supper for you tonight,' exclaimed Tom. 'You deserve it, Samson.'

The sun broke through the clouds and a rainbow shone over the beach.

A few days later, Samson received a letter with a red, wax seal in the post. It read –

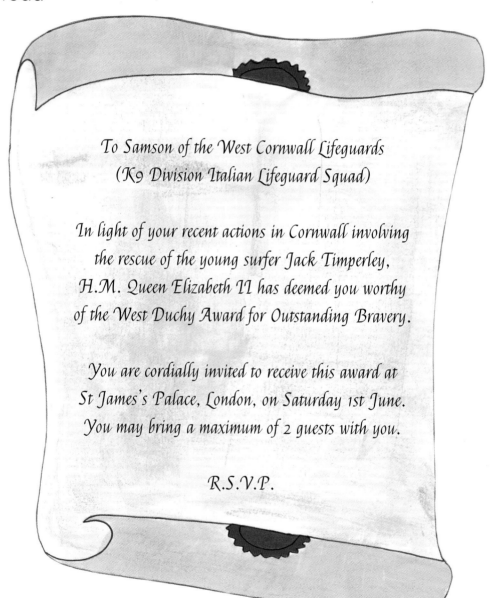

To Samson of the West Cornwall Lifeguards
(K9 Division Italian Lifeguard Squad)

In light of your recent actions in Cornwall involving
the rescue of the young surfer Jack Timperley,
H.M. Queen Elizabeth II has deemed you worthy
of the West Duchy Award for Outstanding Bravery.

You are cordially invited to receive this award at
St James's Palace, London, on Saturday 1st June.
You may bring a maximum of 2 guests with you.

R.S.V.P.

Samson could not believe his eyes when he read the letter. A week later he arrived smartly groomed alongside Tom and John at the Palace. There he met the Queen herself, who placed a shining gold medal around his neck, and thanked all three of the lifeguards for their continuing bravery and dedication in keeping the people on the West Cornwall beaches safe.

THE END

ABOUT THE AUTHOR

Sarah E Webster was born and raised in the Derbyshire Dales. She holds a TA in Lifesaving and was awarded Young Lifesaver of the Year for Derbyshire Branch in 2008 by the Royal Lifesaving Society for her work at her local lifesaving club. She is an avid swimmer who believes that all children should learn about open water safety and should become strong, confident swimmers.